The Poky Little Puppy's First Christmas

By Justine Korman
Illustrated by Jean Chandler

🐿 A GOLDEN BOOK • NEW YORK
Golden Books Publishing Company, Inc., New York, New York 10106

Four little puppies tumbled out of bed one morning and ran to their breakfast bowls. Then they counted themselves: one, two, three, four.

"Now where in the world is that poky little puppy?" they wondered.

Poky was still fast asleep. His mother nudged him and said, "Come on, Poky. Today is Christmas Eve!"

Poky yawned and stretched. Even on a special day like Christmas Eve, he was still poky.

Poky's family, the McCraes, were off to the woods this morning to find a tree, and the puppies were going along, too. Poky ran to catch up.

Then Poky smelled something. He slowed
down to see what it could be.

That's when Poky tumble-stumbled, slipped,
and slid down into a deep, dark hole!
"Help! Help!" he cried. Wouldn't someone
come to help him out of the slippery, slidy hole?

"I'll help you," said a friendly voice. "My name
is Herman."

Poky looked up to see a young skunk peering
over the edge of the hole. Herman climbed down
into the hole beside Poky, and pushed Poky up
and out of the hole.

"You smell funny," said Poky.
Herman sniffed. "You smell funny, too," he said. "Let's play!"

Herman led Poky to a frozen pond, and the two new friends slid back and forth across the cold, shiny ice. What fun!

Over in the woods, the McCraes had found the perfect Christmas tree near a hollow log. Mr. McCrae raised his ax and whack, whack, whacked until—*CRACK!*—the tree fell. The four little puppies barked excitedly.

Poky heard his sister Pickles call, "Poky!
Come on, Poky!" He was sorry to have to say
good-bye to his new friend.

"It's easy to find me," said Herman. "I live in
a hollow log just over that hill."

Poky ran through the snowy woods toward home. Suddenly he saw something. Poky stopped to sniff the strange object up and down.

It was an old red rubber boot. The boot was too wonderful to leave behind, so Poky dragged it all the way home.

"You're late!" Poky's mother scolded gently
when he came through the gate.

"See what I found!" exclaimed Poky.

His mother shook her head and said firmly,
"You can't take that messy, muddy old boot into
the house."

Sadly, Poky left the boot by the garden gate.

After dinner, the puppies helped decorate the Christmas tree.

When the tree was glowing with winking, blinking lights and shimmery glass balls, Poky's mother told her puppies all about Christmas. "And to celebrate this special day, we give each other presents," she said at last. Then she sent the puppies to bed.

Poky, of course, was the last to reach the cozy cushion where the puppies slept.

His brothers and sisters soon fell asleep, dreaming of rubber balls, biscuits, and bones. But Poky stayed awake thinking sadly about his red rubber boot.

On Christmas morning the puppies raced
to the tree—and found presents just for them.
Poky tore open his package. "My boot!" he
cried happily. "And it's all shiny and clean!"

After breakfast a gentle snow began to fall. Poky's brothers and sisters went off to play in the meadow.

"Poky, please don't be late for Christmas dinner," said Poky's mother.

Poky ran out the gate, across the meadow, and into the woods to find Herman.

It took a long time, but Poky finally found Herman. He was wet, cold, and miserable.

"What happened?" asked Poky.

Herman pointed to a crushed hollow log. "That was my home," sniffed Herman. The McCraes had crushed it accidentally when they cut down their Christmas tree.

Poky felt sorry for Herman. The little skunk was alone in the cold, snowy woods, and he had no home. So Poky took Herman home with him.

Poky's mother was surprised to find that her puppy had made friends with a skunk.

But Poky's mother felt sorry for Herman, too. That night she let him sleep in the doghouse she and her puppies shared in the summer.

And Poky gave up his warm, cozy bed in the McCraes' house to keep his friend company.

   The next morning the most amazing thing
happened. The poky little puppy was the first
one out of bed.
   "Where in the world is that poky little
puppy?" everyone wondered.
   The puppies and their mother and Herman
followed Poky's tracks in the cold, crunchy snow.
They went out the gate, across the meadow, and
right to the edge of the wintry woods.
   "Come and look! Look at Herman's new
home!" called Poky.

"Why, it's your boot!" exclaimed Poky's mother.

"Merry Christmas, Herman!" said Poky. "Even
if it is a day late."

Poky's mother was very proud of her puppy.
It was only his first Christmas, but Poky had
already learned that the best gifts of all are the
ones you give.